Monica
and the
Crushworthy
Cowboy

by Diana G. Gallagher

STONE ARCH BOOKS
a capstone imprint

Monica is published by Stone Arch Books
A Capstone Imprint
151 Good Counsel Drive, P.O. Box 669
Mankato, Minnesota 56002
www.capstonepub.com

Printed in the United States of America in Stevens Point, Wisconsin.
032011
006111WZF11

Library of Congress Cataloging-in-Publication Data
Gallagher, Diana G.
  Monica and the crushworthy cowboy / by Diana G. Gallagher.
    p. cm.
  Summary: Thirteen-year-old Monica and her friend Chloe meet a young
cowboy and his friends while on a trip to Kansas City with Monica's
stepfather.
  ISBN-13: 978-1-4342-2554-2 (library binding)
  ISBN-10: 1-4342-2554-2 (library binding)
  1. Cowboys--Juvenile fiction. 2. Rodeos--Juvenile fiction. 3. Stepfathers--
Juvenile fiction. 4. Best friends--Juvenile fiction. 5. Dating (Social customs)
--Juvenile fiction. 6. Kansas City (Mo.)--Juvenile fiction. [1. Cowboys--
Fiction. 2. Rodeos--Fiction. 3. Stepfathers--Fiction. 4. Best friends--Fiction.
5. Dating (Social customs)--Fiction. 6. Kansas City (Mo.)--Fiction.] I. Title.
  PZ7.G13543Mn 2011
  813.54--dc22

                            2011001993

Art Director/Graphic Designer: Kay Fraser
Production Specialist: Michelle Biedscheid

Photo credits:
Cover: Delaney Photography
Avatars: Delaney Photography (Claudia), Shutterstock: Aija Avotina (guitar),
Alex Staroseltsev (baseball), Andrii Muzyka (bowling ball), Anton9 (reptile),
bsites (hat), debra hughes (tree), Dietmar Höpfl (lightning), Dr_Flash (Earth),
Elaine Barker (star), Ivelin Radkov (money), Michael D Brown (smiley face),
Mikhail (horse), originalpunkt (paintbrushes), pixel-pets (dog), R. Gino Santa
Maria (football), Ruth Black (cupcake), Shvaygert Ekaterina (horseshoe),
SPYDER (crown), Tischenko Irina (flower), VectorZilla (clown), Volkova Anna
(heart); Capstone Studio: Karon Dubke (horse Monica, horse Chloe)

-------------------{ table of contents }-------------------

WELCOME BACK, MONICA MURRAY SCREEN NAME: MonicaLuvsHorses

 YOUR AVATAR PICTURE

All updates from your friends

 MONICA MURRAY is making plans for shopping this weekend. Where should we go, Traci Gregory?

 Traci Gregory Let's talk about it at dinner tonight, okay?

 Monica Murray Okay, but I want to map out the day so we hit all my favorite stores!

 Traci Gregory Let's talk about it tonight.

 Monica Murray Okay, okay. See you later.

 LOGAN GREGORY So excited to head to Kansas City this weekend for my first Electrician Trade Show. There are a lot of people I want to meet and lots to learn.

 Mark Bristow There's a rodeo going on this weekend in Kansas City. Think you'll check it out?

 Logan Gregory I'm not a big horse fan. If Monica were coming, I know we'd be going!

 Mark Bristow I bet you'd learn to like it. Enjoy your trade show!

 RORY WEBER to MONICA MURRAY See you at the barn this week?

 Monica Murray For sure!

CHLOE GRANGER to MONICA MURRAY Your stepdad should TOTALLY go to the rodeo. That sounds so cool!

 Monica Murray   I know. Logan isn't crazy about horses, though.

 Chloe Granger   I know, but still!!!

 ANGELA GREGORY has updated her information. She added Shopping to her interests.

 CLAUDIA CORTEZ has invited you to an event: Pool Party at Claudia's! Your current RSVP is: Yes.

Becca McDougal and 4 other people like this.

 Monica Murray   Should I bring chips and dip?

 Claudia Cortez   Sure, that would be good. Get that yummy cheesy kind we like.

 Monica Murray   Okay. See you then! :)

 TRACI GREGORY is excited to spend a special day with a special girl this weekend.

 Angela Gregory   YAY!!! :) :) :) <3

 Monica Murray   Why do you care, Angela?

 Traci Gregory   Let's talk about this at dinner, girls.

 ADAM LOCKE can't wait to hit the pool at Claudia's.

MONICA MURRAY to CHLOE GRANGER Want to come along when my mom and I have our special girls' day on Saturday? We usually shop a lot and get lunch somewhere downtown. You should come!!!

 Chloe Granger   That sounds wonderful!

Chapter One

Special
Saturday

My mom is the banquet manager at the Red Brick Inn. She works nights and weekends, too. **That's why our shopping trips are so important.**

Mom makes special time just for me one Saturday every month. We shop, go out to lunch, and sometimes see a movie if we have time.

I was really excited about the coming weekend. It was our shopping day, and I couldn't wait. And I was hoping that this time, we could take my friend Chloe, too.

Chloe's mom was a doctor. She was always busy working. It would be really fun to include Chloe in my girls' day out with my mom.

On Tuesday, Mom and Logan got home from work just as Grandpa put dinner on the table.

Mom inhaled and smiled. "That smells wonderful!" she said.

"Bet it tastes good, too," Logan said. "I love Grandpa's pepper steak."

"I hate cooked peppers!" Angela said, pretending to gag. "The smell makes me sick."

"I made steak without peppers just for you," Grandpa said. He put a small dish on Angela's plate.

"Thank you," Angela said, smiling sweetly. Then she looked at me and smirked. "You have to eat the yucky stuff."

"I like the yucky stuff," I said.

"No, you don't," Angela said, glaring at me.

I ate a big piece of green pepper.

Angela made a face.

My bratty little stepsister liked me. She just didn't want me to know it.

So she kicked me in the shins, called me names, and blamed me for everything. She used my stuff without asking and broke things on purpose.

If I got mad, she cried. If I got upset, she giggled. If I got even, she did something worse.

But pretending I didn't care drove her nuts. So that's what I usually did.

I gave Mom a few minutes to eat. Then I asked, "Can Chloe go shopping with us next Saturday?"

"I'd love to take Chloe," Mom said. "But we'll have to do it next month. I'm taking Angela out to shop and eat this Saturday."

"Just the two of us,"

Angela said with a smug grin.

I was speechless, outraged, and hurt.

My one Saturday a month was the only time I didn't have to compete with Logan and my stepsister for Mom's attention.

I wasn't going to give it up without a fight.

"Wouldn't you rather go to the movies?" I asked.

"No," Angela answered.

"Angela asked to go shopping," Mom said.

"And out to lunch at the Red Brick Inn," Angela added.

Aha! It was Angela's idea. That really made me mad. Angela only wanted to go on a shopping-lunch trip because it was my special thing to do with my mother.

It wouldn't be special if Angela did it too!

I wanted to say so, but Mom looked so happy. So I didn't.

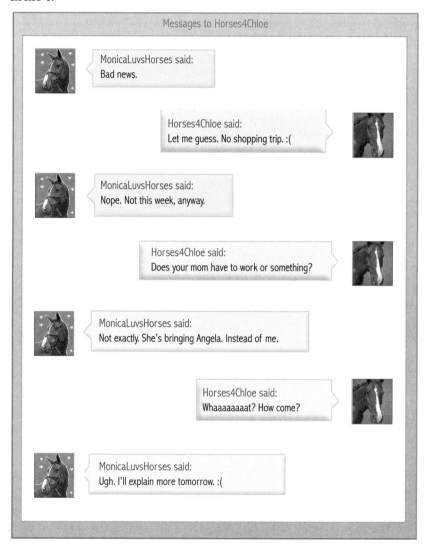

"Don't look so down, Monica," Grandpa said. "You have other things to do next Saturday."

I nodded. "Sure," I said. "Season Four of *Bridle Village* is streaming online now."

"I have a better idea," Logan said.

I frowned. "What?" I asked.

"I'm going to a trade show in Kansas City next weekend," Logan said. "Would you like to go?"

I squealed. "Yes!" I said.

"Great!" Logan said. He grinned. "It'll give me a chance to spend some special time with you."

"But you're my daddy!" Angela wailed. "I want to go too!"

Chapter Two

Why Girls Need a
Mom

Angela wouldn't listen to reason when she was mad. Logan tried anyway.

"You can't go this time, Angela," he said. "I'll take you somewhere when you're thirteen."

"I want to go now!" Angela yelled. She threw her fork down. She stuck out her lower lip, folded her arms, and pouted.

Mom, Logan, Grandpa, and I all looked at each other. We weren't new to Angela's brat attacks. There were a few things we could do to make them stop.

We tried ignoring her.

"Pass the potatoes, please," Grandpa said.

"Here you go," Logan said, handing over the bowl.

"Did you get a room at the Royal?" Mom asked Logan.

"What's the Royal?" I asked.

"A very nice hotel in downtown Kansas City," Logan said.

"I want to go to Kansas City!" Angela screeched. Then she burst into tears.

Mom, Logan, Grandpa, and I looked at each other again. I'm pretty sure we were all remembering that Angela never backed down once she set her mind on something.

"I was looking forward to shopping with you next Saturday," Traci said. "Don't you want a new dress?"

"No," Angela said. She wiped her nose and banged her shoes on her chair.

Mom had forgotten that Angela was impossible to bribe.

MonicaLuvsHorses said:
Guess what? Logan's taking me to Kansas City next weekend!!!

ClaudiaCristina said:
Fun! What are you going to do there?

MonicaLuvsHorses said:
I don't know, but I'm sure he has something planned for us to do.

ClaudiaCristina said:
Are your mom and Angela going too?

MonicaLuvsHorses said:
Nope. Just me.

ClaudiaCristina said:
You'll have a blast. Will it be weird spending time with Logan without your mom or Angela?

MonicaLuvsHorses said:
I don't think so. He's not embarrassing, most of the time, and he usually lets me do my own thing.

ClaudiaCristina said:
I'm jealous! :) Send me a postcard.

"Okay, I think it's time for bed," Logan said.

"I don't want to go to bed!" Angela yelled. "I want to go to Kansas City!" She jumped up and ran out of the room.

Logan went after her. Mom followed Logan.

I volunteered to do the dishes so that Grandpa could read the newspaper and relax.

He couldn't watch TV. Angela was still screaming.

* * *

After Angela calmed down, Logan came into the kitchen to help me. He rinsed and I loaded the dishwasher.

"That was pretty crazy, huh?" he said.

"Yeah. Is she in bed?" I asked.

Logan shook his head. "She's taking a bubble bath," he told me.

"Is that why she stopped screaming?" I asked.

"No," Logan said. "She decided she didn't want to go to Kansas City after all."

I was shocked. "Why did she change her mind?" I asked.

"I pointed out that going out to lunch with Traci will be way more fun than looking at electrical supplies all day," Logan said.

I blinked. "Is that what we're going to do?" I asked. "Look at electrical supplies?"

"Well, at least part of the time. It's a business trip for me," Logan explained. "I have to check out the new products at the trade show and talk to the people that sell them."

My stepdad was **the manager of Granite Electric**. He had to know about plugs, wires, and switches for his job.

I was a teenage girl. I never thought about plugs and switches unless important stuff like lights and TV stopped working.

"Some of the displays are interesting," Logan said.

Mom overheard when she walked in. I shot her a look, and she said what I was thinking.

"Oh, Logan. Monica will be bored to death at the show," Mom said.

"She doesn't have to stay at the trade show," Logan explained. He put the leftover pepper steak in the refrigerator. "She can watch movies in the hotel room or wander around the Plaza."

"What's the Plaza?" I asked.

"A famous shopping district in downtown Kansas City," Mom explained. "The Plaza has lots of restaurants and boutiques. You'll love it. I promise."

"And horse-drawn carriage rides," Logan added. "Which should be right up your alley."

"Oh, I can't wait to see that!" I said. "We can go shopping and out to lunch on Saturday, too!"

Logan frowned and glanced at my mom. "Um, actually . . . I'll be busy during the day on Saturday, Monica," he said.

I stopped smiling. "I don't want to see the Plaza by myself," I said. "That sounds kind of lonely."

"I'll take you," Logan said. "I just don't know when."

"Take Chloe with you," Mom suggested. "Then the girls could hang out together."

That was an amazing idea! I knew Chloe and I would have a fantastic time, and it would feel like a really exciting vacation. Not just tagging along to a trade show with my stepdad.

"Could we?" I asked. I clasped my hands and begged. "Please, please, please!"

Logan ran his hand over his head. Then he exhaled. He does that when he's not sure about something.

"They wouldn't be bored, and it would be much safer," Mom added.

"I know," Logan said, "but I only have two tickets to the rodeo."

"The rodeo!" I squealed. "Chloe would love to see a rodeo!"

"Being there would be so much better than getting texts from Monica," Mom said.

"All right!" Logan said. He threw up his hands. Then he smiled. "Chloe can go."

"Thanks, Logan!" I said. I threw my arms around him.

Logan sighed. "I hope I can get another rodeo ticket," he said.

Chapter Three

Don't Fall for a
Cowboy

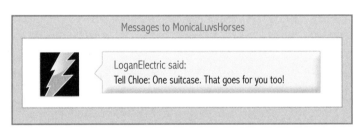

Messages to MonicaLuvsHorses

LoganElectric said:
Tell Chloe: One suitcase. That goes for you too!

Chloe and I met at the barn on Thursday. We took Rick-Rack and Lancelot out on the trails for a goodbye ride.

"I still can't believe Logan invited me to go with you!" Chloe exclaimed.

"I had to beg," I said.

"No, you didn't," Chloe said.

"Just a little," I told her. "He's pretty cool."

My real dad got sick and died when I was seven.

Logan was the next best thing.

He made me feel loved and safe, and I liked him a lot. And I definitely loved how happy my mom was with him.

"I can't wait to see the Plaza," Chloe said. "I looked it up online. The sidewalks are like gardens with benches and fountains. We can rest in style between stores, and sip cappuccinos or something."

"Or go for a carriage ride," I said.

"Then shop some more," Chloe said.

"And have lunch at a super classy restaurant," I added.

"And go shopping again," Chloe finished. She laughed.

"Definitely shopping!" I said, grinning. "Lots and lots of shopping."

Then I got serious. "But Logan wants us to see the trade show, too," I said. "Just for a little while. Some of the displays might be interesting, but mostly it's just electrical parts and stuff. I think he just wants me to see what he does."

"I don't mind going for a little while," Chloe said. "He's taking us to the rodeo, and he doesn't like horses."

That's how I felt. I wasn't even worried about looking bored and hurting Logan's feelings. After all, I was already good at pretending to love his favorite baseball movies, old cars, and football.

"What clothes are you taking?" Chloe asked.

"I can't decide," I said. "Everything I might need won't fit in one suitcase, but Logan said we can only bring one each."

"One isn't enough," Chloe said.

"Not when we have to be ready for anything," I said.

"Should I pack a dress-up outfit?" Chloe asked.

"I am," I said. "In case we go to a fancy restaurant for dinner."

"I hope I have room!" Chloe exclaimed. "I'm already bringing two bathing suits. I looked at the website. The hotel pool is open late, so we might go more than once in one day, and I hate putting on wet suits."

"Oooh, good thinking," I said.

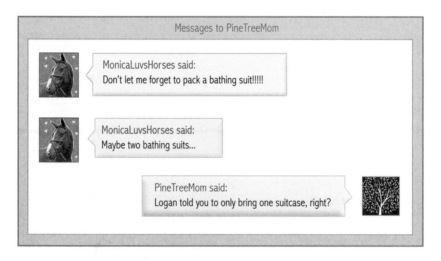

Messages to PineTreeMom

MonicaLuvsHorses said:
Don't let me forget to pack a bathing suit!!!!!

MonicaLuvsHorses said:
Maybe two bathing suits...

PineTreeMom said:
Logan told you to only bring one suitcase, right?

"This is going to be awesome," Chloe said. "I can't wait."

"Me too," I said. Then I leaned over and patted Lancelot's head. "But I'm going to miss you, buddy," I said, scratching him behind his ears.

"We'll be back soon. And breaks are good for horses," Chloe said. Then she smiled. "But I'm going to miss Rick-Rack, too!" She gave her horse a little nuzzle. "I hope Rory takes good care of you!"

Teenage gossip traveled fast, especially at the barn where Chloe and I took riding lessons. By the time Chloe and I got back from our ride, everybody at Rock Creek Stables knew that Chloe and I were going to the rodeo in Kansas City.

Megan and Lydia ambushed us in the tack room. "Oh, look," Megan exclaimed sarcastically. "It's Chloe and Monica!"

"Are you excited about going to the rodeo?" Lydia asked. "I never want to go to one."

"Western horses are too short, and the saddles are too big," Megan added. She wrinkled her nose. "And cowboys are scruffy."

"Some people think those rodeo guys are romantic," Rory said as he walked in.

"They tackle cows!" Megan said. She rolled her eyes and pulled Lydia out the door.

"Why does Megan try to spoil everything?" Chloe asked.

"She doesn't want anyone to enjoy something she doesn't have," Rory said. "Believe me. She'd love to go to a big regional rodeo."

"And date a rodeo rider," I said.

"Cowboys are exciting," Chloe said.

"And cute," I added.

"Don't fall for a cowboy, Monica," Rory said. "They break broncos and hearts."

I laughed.

But inside, I knew that if I really let myself fall for Rory, he could break my heart.

Chapter Four

On the
Road

Messages to Horses4Chloe

MonicaLuvsHorses said:
Be ready tomorrow morning at 3:30!!!

Horses4Chloe said:
I will be. But it's soooooo early!

MonicaLuvsHorses said:
I know. We can sleep in the car.

Mom shook me awake at 3 a.m. on Friday morning. I was still yawning when Logan and I left at 3:15. We picked Chloe up at 3:30. She was wide awake.

We were both surprised when Logan opened the trunk to load our suitcases. There was plenty of room! We could have fit at least three more suitcases in there, easily.

I didn't want to complain, but I had to ask. "Why couldn't we bring more than one suitcase?" I asked Logan. "The trunk isn't even half full."

"We'll only be gone for three days," Logan said. "You don't need more than you can pack in one suitcase."

Chloe raised an eyebrow. My mouth fell open.

"I only brought one," Logan added, pointing to his small suitcase.

"You're a guy!" I exclaimed. "All you need is a suit, jeans, and some shirts."

"And you can dress to go anywhere," Chloe said.

"It's not that easy for girls," I said. "We need different outfits for everything."

"Like what?" Logan asked.

"Sweaters and sneakers if it's cold," Chloe said. "Shorts and sandals if it's hot."

"School clothes for the trade show," I added. "Jeans and boots for the rodeo."

"A dozen different tops and a dress with heels," Chloe said.

"Bathing suits, pajamas, slippers, and a robe," I went on, counting off on my fingers.

"And hair and bathroom stuff," Chloe finished.

"Did you get all that into one suitcase?" Logan asked. He sounded amazed.

"Yes, but it wasn't easy," I said.

"Everything's squished," Chloe said. "I had to wear my boots."

"Me too," I said.

"Well, I'm glad you worked it out," Logan said. "Anyway, I need room in the trunk for samples and supplies on the trip home."

I dropped the subject when we got back into the car.

"If you're tired, you can go back to sleep," Logan said.

"I'm too excited," Chloe said.

"I'm hungry," I admitted. My stomach growled. It wasn't used to being awake in the middle of the night.

Logan stopped at a 24-hour fast-food restaurant. He ordered breakfast sandwiches for everyone. He drank coffee. Chloe and I sipped OJ.

"When will we get there?" I asked.

"Around noon," Logan said.

"Can we go to the Plaza after lunch?" Chloe asked.

"Not today," Logan said. "I have to be at the trade show all afternoon."

Chloe and I looked at each other. We really didn't want to spend our first day at the trade show.

"Are we going with you?" I asked.

"You can stay at the hotel," Logan said. "I'll take you for a quick tour tomorrow."

Chloe and I relaxed.

"Can we order room service?" I asked.

"Sure," Logan said. "You can watch movies or go to the pool. The hotel also has a game room and gift shop."

"Awesome!" Chloe said. She grinned.

"Just don't go anywhere alone," Logan said. "Stay together."

Chloe and I promised.

Then we fell asleep listening to music on our MP3 players. We woke up when Logan drove over a large bridge. The grooved road rattled the tires.

"Almost there," Logan said.

The highway followed the river. Then it curved around the tall buildings in the center of the city.

"Welcome to the big city, girls," Logan said.

"Kansas City isn't as big as New York City," Chloe said. "We went there on vacation last year."

"Did you stay in a fancy hotel?" I asked.

Chloe shrugged. "It wasn't that fancy," she said. "But it was cool."

"Here we are," Logan announced as he pulled into a circular driveway. "The Royal Hotel."

"Fantastic!"
Chloe said. She grinned.

I tried not to look too impressed when a valet opened the car door. A bellman loaded our bags onto a cart. Then the valet drove the car away to park it.

The lobby looked like the elegant hotels I saw on TV. A crystal chandelier hung from the high ceiling. Groups of sofas, chairs, and tables were placed here and there. Palm trees, ferns, and flowers grew in large pots and planters. An adorable café was set up by the huge front windows.

"Can we eat lunch there?" I asked. The café would be more fun than room service.

"You and Chloe can," Logan said. "Right after we check in. I have to get to the trade show, but you can charge lunch to our room."

Our room was on the twenty-first floor. The express elevator went so fast it made my stomach feel like I was on a rollercoaster.

"Wow!" I exclaimed when we walked into our room. It wasn't just a room. It was a suite with two bedrooms and a sitting room.

"This is way better than the hotel in New York," Chloe said.

"Pick a room," Logan said.

Chloe and I couldn't control our excitement any longer. We shrieked, ran into a bedroom, and flopped on the beds.

"No jumping on the beds!" Logan yelled.

"You never let us have any fun!" I teased.

We all laughed.

Chapter Five

Pool Party

Chloe and I unpacked quickly. It wasn't hard. There was lots of room in the closet and dresser. We had our own bathroom, too. Chloe put her stuff on one side of the sink. I used the other.

We took the express elevator back downstairs for lunch. It made my stomach feel weird again. But I was definitely hungry by the time we got to the café.

Our table was outside, on the stone patio. Chloe and I sipped water out of heavy goblets. We pretended to be fancy ladies at lunch. And I felt very important when I told the waiter to charge the meal to our room.

Once we were done eating, Chloe said, "Is it time to hit the pool?"

"Absolutely," I said. "Let's go!"

We headed up to our room to change. Then we went back down the elevator to the pool.

The outdoor pool was on the third floor. Large glass doors opened up onto a patio. We picked two lounge chairs near the hot tub and spread our big fluffy towels out in the sun.

"Do you want a soda?" Chloe asked.

"I'd love one," I said. I gave Chloe money for the vending machine. Then I leaned back and closed my eyes.

No one else was at the pool. It was so quiet and warm, and I was so tired, that I dozed off.

"Are you asleep?" Chloe asked when she came back.

I sat up with a start. "Oh! Um, yeah. I guess I fell asleep. Did I miss something?" I asked.

"Almost," Chloe said. She handed me a soda and sat down. "We've got company."

I looked up. Three guys around our age, or maybe a little older, were in the pool. A girl was sitting on the edge, dangling her feet in the water. She smiled when she caught us staring.

"Come on in!" one of the boys yelled and waved at us. "The water's warm!"

Chloe and I looked at each other. She shrugged. "We might as well," she said.

"Okay," I said. We got up and headed over to the pool.

We sat down by the girl, and the boys swam over.

"I'm Jillian Wheeler," the girl said. "This is my brother, Jon." She gently shoved the shortest guy with her foot. **"He's thireen and totally obnoxious."**

"She's fourteen, and she's just mad because she's not an only child," Jon said. He looked at me and smiled. "I'm only a little obnoxious."

I grinned. "I'm Monica Murray," I told them, "and this is Chloe Granger."

"Hi," Chloe said.

"Cory Slade," said the cute, tall blond boy. He shook hands with Chloe. "I hope you don't think I'm obnoxious."

"Hmm. It's too soon to tell," Chloe said. She winked. Then she slipped into the pool.

"Who wants to play Marco Polo?" the third boy asked. He seemed older than the other two. He grabbed Jillian's leg and pulled her into the water. Then he looked at me.

"I'm Bobby," he said. "Nice to meet you."

"I'll get you for that, Bobby!" Jillian said, coming up for air. She laughed and splashed him.

Then everyone looked at me. I was the only one who wasn't wet!

"Come on in, Monica!" Chloe said.

I jumped in.

"You're it, Jon!" Jillian yelled.

Jon didn't argue. He closed his eyes and started counting to ten. Everyone scattered.

"Marco!" Jon yelled.

"Polo!" we all yelled back.

Jon hesitated, then called out again. "Marco!"

The third time, he turned right toward me! I tried to keep out of his way, but he started swimming right for me.

"Gotcha, Monica!" Jon said. He grinned when he tagged me. "You're it."

I tagged Bobby when he tried to sneak up behind me.

Bobby went after Jillian right away. It was obvious that they liked each other.

When we got out of the water, Cory helped Chloe bring our towels and drinks to their table. Jon brought two more chairs over to the table, one for him and one for me.

I didn't mind the attention. Jon wasn't quite as cute as Rory, but he was nice. And cute enough.

"So, Monica. Are you here for the rodeo?" Jon asked me.

"My stepdad is here for a trade show," I said. "Chloe and I came along for the ride. We have tickets for the rodeo tomorrow night."

"Are you guys going?" Chloe asked.

"We have to be there," Bobby said. "We're all competing tomorrow and Sunday."

"Wow!" I exclaimed. "That's fantastic!"

"You must be really good," Chloe said.

"We have great trainers," Cory explained. "Ty and Joann. They're Jillian and Jon's mom and dad."

"Also, we practice a lot," Jillian said. "My parents gave us the afternoon off to relax."

"I'm impressed," I said.

"Good," Jon said. "Maybe you'll bring me luck."

"Bobby wrestles steers," Jillian said.

"It's called bulldogging," Bobby said.

"What do you do, Cory?" Chloe asked.

"Calf roping," Cory answered. "Jillian is a barrel racer."

"I've never had the guts to try that," Chloe said. "It looks like the horse might fall over."

That's how it looked to me, too. In barrel racing, the horse ran a cloverleaf pattern around three barrels. It leaned in as it turned to save time. The fastest horse was the winner.

"I'm not the bravest rider. I've never had the guts to try jumping a fence that's as tall as my horse!" Jillian exclaimed.

"I've never jumped that high," I said.

"Me either. But I'd like to someday," Chloe said.

"You guys ride?" Jon asked.

I nodded. "We ride jumpers and hunters," I explained. "Not really the same thing."

"That's cool," Jon said.

"That's *really* cool," Jillian said. "So you guys totally get it."

Chloe and I looked at each other and smiled. "I guess we do," she said.

"I want to win a champion belt buckle," Cory said. "Jon's dad has four."

"That is so cool!" I exclaimed. "Was your mom a rodeo rider too, Jillian?"

"She was a trick rider," Jillian said. "Now she helps Dad with our training."

"But they don't push us to win, or anything," Jon quickly added. "They told us that we have to do this for ourselves, not for them."

"They push me!" Cory joked.

"That's because you're good and want to break records," Bobby said. "I ride for fun."

"Hey, we're having dinner in the hotel café tonight," Jillian said. "Maybe you two can come too. And your stepdad, of course."

Chloe looked at me and nodded. She wanted to go.

"What time?" I asked. I just hoped Logan hadn't made other plans.

Messages to MonicaLuvsHorses

Guitar_Rory said:
Hey you. How's your trip going?

MonicaLuvsHorses said:
Great!

Guitar_Rory said:
What have you been doing?

MonicaLuvsHorses said:
Oh, you know. Just hanging out. The hotel is amazing!

Guitar_Rory said:
Sweet. :) Have a great time...

Chapter Six

Bad
Dad

I wasn't positive Jon liked me until we got to the café. He saved me a seat. Cory saved one for Chloe. I was pretty sure the big smiles they gave us were clues that they saw us as more than just new friends.

The Wheelers were very nice. Logan liked them right away.

"Just call us Ty and Joann," Jon's father said. "You too, kids. Mr. Wheeler sounds like an old man, even if I am."

"You're not that old," Joann said.

"I am for a rodeo rider," Ty said.

"I hear you were a champion," Logan said.

"Four times All Round Cowboy," Bobby said.

Jon beamed with pride. "Dad roped calves and rode bulls and broncs bareback," he said.

"Joann was a trick rider," I said.

"That sounds exciting," Logan said. But he didn't seem all that excited. I was starting to feel nervous. Luckily, just then a waiter walked over to take our order.

"What business are you in, Logan?" Joann asked once we'd all ordered.

"I'm in electrical installation and repair," Logan told her.

"What do you do at a trade show?" Jon asked.

"Oh, mostly look at new products and try to get low prices," Logan answered. "It's mostly to meet people and network."

I knew that the trade show was a bigger deal than that! Logan was the manager at Granite Electric. He had to make sure the company used good materials, and he had to keep costs down.

But before I could brag about my stepfather, Jillian asked him, "Do you ride?"

"Horses?" Logan asked. He shook his head. "No. Watching Monica ride is close enough for me."

Logan didn't like horses. He and my mom paid for my lessons because they knew it was important to me. He didn't know much about horse stuff, and that was mostly what we talked about at dinner.

He acted like he was interested, but I knew Logan. He was just being polite.

"We're going to see *Raven's Revenge* after dinner," Jillian said. "Can Monica and Chloe go with us?"

Chloe and I looked at Logan. Logan hesitated.

"Can we?" I asked.

"Everyone I know wants to see that movie," Chloe said.

"I've been waiting since *Raven's Rise* came out two years ago," Jon said.

"The theater's on the next block," Joann said. "Our kids go to the movies alone all the time."

"We trust them," Ty added. "If they get into trouble, they know they won't go again."

I knew Logan wasn't comfortable letting Chloe and me go out alone. But he also knew that we'd be totally embarrassed if he said no. I hoped that would make a difference.

"Please?" I said.

Logan sighed. "Okay, you can go," he said. "I have to organize my notes before my meetings tomorrow."

I was so surprised and so happy I hugged him.

* * *

An hour later, I wanted to kill Logan.

Jillian, Bobby, Chloe, Cory, Jon, and I were sitting in a row at the theater. Chloe sat between Cory and me. Jon was on my other side.

About halfway through the movie, Chloe went to get more popcorn. When she came back, she leaned over and whispered, "Logan's here."

"What?" I whispered back. "What are you talking about?"

Chloe pointed toward the back of the theater. "He's here," she repeated. "He's sitting two rows behind us."

Chapter Seven

Scared
of What?

We stopped to look at posters after the movie, and everyone saw Logan leaving the theater. It was pretty obvious that I was embarrassed, but nobody said a word. I couldn't believe he'd followed us.

When we got back to the hotel, Logan was talking to Ty and Joann in the lobby.

"If Jillian was out with strange kids, I would have followed her, too," Ty said.

"You were just being a responsible parent," Joann said. "I'm sure Monica understands." She looked at me. "Right, Monica?"

I did understand, but that didn't change how I felt. I resented being treated like a baby.

"Yeah," I said. "I get it."

"I'm sorry, Monica," Logan said. "But I had to make sure you were safe."

"Yeah. I know," I said.

"Are you busy tomorrow?" Cory asked Chloe.

"We're going to the Plaza," Chloe said.

"When?" Jon asked.

"That depends on how long I'll be at the trade show," Logan said. "I might be tied up all day."

"The girls could go to the rodeo with us," Joann said. "Jillian rides in the morning."

"That would be great!" Jillian exclaimed. "Then you'll see what rodeo is like first hand."

"Seriously?" I asked.

"That would be amazing!" Chloe whispered.

"We can always use extra help," Ty said.

"We'll be with them all day," Joann added.

Logan frowned, like he had to think hard to decide. Then he grinned. "They're all yours," he said.

"Breakfast in the café at seven on the dot," Joann told us.

Ty gave Logan a barn pass so he could find us after the trade show. Then we headed upstairs.

"Want to watch a movie with us?" I asked Logan as we rode up in the elevator. I wanted him to know I wasn't mad anymore.

"I wish I could," Logan said. "But I went to the movie instead of doing my work. So I can't."

"Oh. Okay," I said.

When we got to our suite, Chloe and I went into our bedroom and closed the door.

"Now we know why Rory warned you to watch out for cowboys," Chloe said, smiling.

"Cory and Jon are so nice," I said.

"Exactly." Chloe grinned again. "And adorable."

"And talented," I added.

"And they really like us," Chloe said.

"Maybe," I said, frowning. "I can't tell. I kind of thought the movie would be more like a date. But it wasn't."

"Yeah, Cory didn't even put his arm around me," Chloe said. "Did you want Jon to?"

"No!" I exclaimed. "I would have pulled away if he put his arm around me."

"Why?" Chloe asked.

I shrugged. But Chloe didn't give up. "It's because you like Rory, and you just don't want to admit it. Right?" she asked.

"Is there something wrong with me?" I asked, flopping onto my bed.

"Like what?" Chloe asked, puzzled.

"I don't know," I said. "Why didn't Jon want to hold hands or kiss me or anything?"

"Logan was there," Chloe said.

"Jon didn't know that until we left," I reminded her.

"Maybe Cory and Jon are just scared," she said.

I laughed. "Of what?" I asked.

"Girls," Chloe said. "Cory freaked out when our knees touched!"

Chapter Eight

Racer, Rider, Runaway

Getting ready for a rodeo was just like getting ready for a horse show. Chloe and I helped. All morning, we filled water buckets, polished saddles, and brushed horses.

Barrel racing was the first event. When it was time, Ty, Joann, and Bobby walked Jillian to the staging area.

Cory and Jon took Chloe and me to the huge indoor arena. We sat in the exhibitor seats, and the boys explained barrel racing again.

"The fastest horse wins," Jon told us.

"But you can't knock down a barrel or mess up the pattern," Cory added.

Jon pointed at two posts spaced several feet apart. "That's the start and finish line," he said. "The timer starts and stops when the horse goes between the posts."

I watched the first few riders closely. The horses that stayed close to the barrels had faster times.

"Here we go," Jon said when Jillian entered the ring.

Jillian's horse was ready.

MoJo exploded into a gallop when she kicked him forward. He was still going full speed after he rounded all three barrels. A horn blared when they crossed the finish line.

"Thirty point three seconds," the announcer said.

"Yeehaw!" Jon yelled. He waved his hat.

One horse was faster, and Jillian came in second. Still, that was fantastic for a big rodeo. Everyone was thrilled.

"That was really great. Barrel racing looks like fun," Chloe said when Jillian walked back over to us.

"Do you want to try it?" Jillian asked us.

"Yes!" Chloe and I answered.

Jillian took us to the outside warm-up area. The practice barrels were still set up. Chloe and I each rode the course twice, but we didn't go very fast. Barrel racing was just as scary as it looked.

Chloe grinned as she dismounted. "The next time Megan and Lydia make fun of us, let's challenge them to a barrel race!" she said.

"Ha!" I said. "That sounds like a great idea."

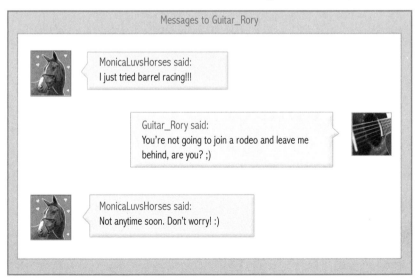

Messages to Guitar_Rory

MonicaLuvsHorses said:
I just tried barrel racing!!!

Guitar_Rory said:
You're not going to join a rodeo and leave me behind, are you? ;)

MonicaLuvsHorses said:
Not anytime soon. Don't worry! :)

Chloe went to get us some snacks. I found the boys where we'd left them.

"So, my bronc-riding event is up next," Jon told me.

"Cool!" I said. "I can't wait to watch."

"So. I've been wondering. Can I have a kiss for luck?" Jon asked.

Without even thinking about it, I said, "No!" and stepped back.

Jon looked so disappointed I felt sorry for him. So instead of kissing him, I took a dollar from my pocket and kissed that. "For luck," I said, smiling.

"Oh. Thanks a lot," Jon said. He smiled and added, "My lucky charm." He put the folded bill in his pocket. Then he winked at me and walked away.

I felt kind of stupid.

A really cute, really nice guy wanted to kiss me, and I didn't want to kiss him back. What was wrong with me?

When he asked if he could kiss me, all I could think about was Rory.

When Chloe came back from the bathroom, I decided not to tell her what had happened.

Soon, Chloe and I were settled in our seats. Jillian sat down next to us. "Can you tell us about bronc riding?" I asked. "I don't know much about it."

"Well, the riders hold onto the strap with one hand," Jillian said. "They can't touch the horse with their other hand."

"How do you know who wins?" I asked.

"You have to stay on for eight seconds. Then you get scored from zero to fifty points," Jillian said. "The horse is scored, too. A bronc that twists and bucks hard gets more points."

The riders went in one by one. Chloe and I winced every time someone got bucked off. A lot of riders stayed on for the whole eight seconds. After the horn sounded, cowboys on horses helped the riders get off safely.

"There's Jon!" Jillian said. She pointed toward the chutes.

Jon looked grim as he gripped the strap.

My heart leaped into my throat when the chute opened and the bronc burst out. The horse twisted and kicked, bucked and spun, but Jon stayed on. We all cheered.

"And that's an 83 for Jon Wheeler," the announcer said.

I frowned. "That's not as high as some of the others," I said.

"But it's better than most," Jillian said. "Jon will be happy he did so well."

We saw Logan walking toward us when we got back to the barn area. He was checking stall numbers.

"Logan!" I called, waving.

Logan waved back. He looked relieved to see us. "Are you and Chloe ready to go to the Plaza?" Logan asked. "I'll take you to my favorite restaurant for dinner."

"I forgot you were going to the Plaza," Jillian said.

Chloe and I exchanged another look. We were having so much fun that we had forgotten, too.

"We kind of made plans to go swimming," I said.

"Oh," Logan said. He nodded, but he sighed.

Suddenly, I felt awful. Logan brought me to Kansas City so that we could spend time together. I had spent most of my time with Chloe and our new friends. I had to fix that. Quick!

"But I'd rather go shopping with you," I said.

"So would I," Chloe said. She smiled at me.

"Me, too," Jillian blurted out. She turned red and added, "Sometimes a cowgirl just wants to be a girl."

"Then you should come with us, Jillian," Logan said. "I'll go clear it with your parents."

"Your stepdad is pretty cool," Jillian said after Logan walked away.

"I know," I said.

Jillian grinned. "I wish my dad knew more about teenage girls," she admitted.

Chapter Nine

Girls' Day
Out

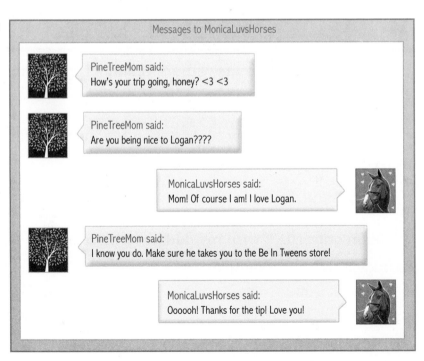

Messages to MonicaLuvsHorses

PineTreeMom said:
How's your trip going, honey? <3 <3

PineTreeMom said:
Are you being nice to Logan????

MonicaLuvsHorses said:
Mom! Of course I am! I love Logan.

PineTreeMom said:
I know you do. Make sure he takes you to the Be In Tweens store!

MonicaLuvsHorses said:
Oooooh! Thanks for the tip! Love you!

Chloe, Jillian, and I window-shopped for hours. Logan wasn't interested in clothes, but he waited patiently until we moved on. So we didn't complain when Logan stopped at the Electronics Universe window display.

"That's what I want for my birthday," Logan said, pointing at some weird gadget. "A pocket satellite TV. Tell your mom." He winked at me.

I gasped when I looked at the price sticker. "It costs nine hundred dollars!" I said.

"I'll chip in," Logan joked.

When I spotted Be In Tweens, I smiled at Logan. "You might want to buy a newspaper," I told him. "We'll be here a while."

Logan took my advice. He sat in a comfy chair and read the *Kansas City Star* while we tried on clothes.

Messages to MonicaLuvsHorses

LoganElectric said:
You can pick out an outfit if you want. My treat.

MonicaLuvsHorses said:
Really???? THANKS!!! Love you!

Everything I tried on looked great, but it was all really expensive. I didn't think Logan knew what he was getting into. So instead of picking out an outfit, I chose gloves that matched my Ginger Snap bag. They would be perfect when it got cold out.

Chloe bought a star-shaped charm for her silver bracelet. Jillian found the perfect dress for a school dance she was going to back at home.

We were all starved when we finished. "Are you hungry?" Logan asked.

I nodded. "We should get some BBQ," I said. "Everyone says it's the best here."

Logan slapped his forehead. "Kansas City is famous for BBQ! Glad you thought of it, Monica."

At the restaurant, Logan asked for a table in the courtyard. We all ordered barbequed ribs with French fries and sweet coleslaw. The food was so good I ate every single bite.

"I'm stuffed," Chloe groaned when we were finished.

"Too stuffed for cheesecake?" Logan asked.

"I'll make room for that!" Chloe said, grinning.

"Eat up," Logan said. "We'd better hurry. We've got three tickets for the rodeo tonight."

"Oh!" Jillian said. "I thought you guys could sit with us in the exhibitor seats."

"That sounds amazing!" I said. Chloe nodded.

Then I saw the hurt look on Logan's face.

"Of course," Logan said. He smiled tightly.

"We don't know anything about rodeo," Chloe explained. "Jillian can answer all our questions."

"You're invited too," Jillian told him.

"Thank you, but I'll pass," Logan said. "There are other things I can do tonight."

I didn't believe him.

Chapter Ten

All Logan's Fault

Logan called me about twenty minutes after Chloe and I got to the rodeo. I didn't hear my phone ring, but I listened to the voicemail.

Logan sounded happy. "Good news!" he said. "I was just, um, wandering around at the trade show, and I overheard someone saying they tried to get tickets to the rodeo. Turns out it's a guy I know, Warren Schwartz. He owns an electrical supply business, and we've worked together before. Anyway, he and his kid, Mitchell, are going to go with me tonight. So if you were feeling bad, please don't. I'll try to find you at the rodeo. See you later. Have fun."

That was a huge relief. I had been feeling bad. Now I could just relax and enjoy the rodeo.

But Chloe wasn't relaxed. While we watched everyone getting ready, she was worrying about Bobby's bulldogging event the next day. "Steers are so big! Isn't wrestling them dangerous?" she asked.

"Nope," Bobby said. He grinned. "Cowboys always win, and steers don't hold a grudge."

Everyone laughed, except Cory. He just looked nervous.

"Riders get points at every rodeo," Ty said. "The Rodeo Association adds them up and keeps track."

"If Cory wins tomorrow, he'll be Regional Champion," Joann explained.

Cory was too nervous to sit. "Hey, Chloe, let's go get hotdogs for everyone," he suggested.

Chloe smiled. "Okay," she said. She smiled at me as she and Cory walked away.

A few minutes later, Logan brought his guests over to meet us.

"Mitchell is having a great time," Mr. Schwartz said, pointing at his son. "He wants to be a cowboy."

"I want to be a rodeo rider," Mitchell said. "Just like Jesse Thomas. He's the best. He's a National Rodeo Champion!"

"Jesse is an old friend of mine," Ty said. "Would you like to meet him?"

"Yes!" Mitchell said. He looked thrilled.

Ty and Jillian took Mitchell to find Jesse. Logan and Mr. Schwartz stayed behind to talk to Joann. Mr. Schwartz had lots of questions about rodeo life.

"Mitchell is only eight," Joann said. "He might change his mind about wanting to ride broncos when he grows up."

"That will be up to him," Mr. Schwartz said.

I smiled. I knew that Logan and Mom felt the same way about me. Even before I'd ever ridden a horse, I'd always wanted to be an Olympic rider or a jockey. They just wanted me to be happy.

"Dad! Look!" Mitchell yelled. He broke away from Ty and Jillian, walking back to us. He ran toward us, waving a photo of Jesse Thomas.

Cory and Chloe were coming back with boxes of hotdogs at the same time. Mitchell ran right in front of them.

Cory stumbled and tripped. He tried to save the hotdogs, but he fell on his arm.

Everyone rushed over. "Are you okay?" Ty asked, kneeling down next to Cory.

"My wrist hurts," Cory said. He winced when he moved his hand.

Joann reached over and gently felt his wrist. "It's not broken," she said.

"That's great news!" Chloe said hopefully.

"A sprain could be just as bad," Ty said. "Cory needs two good wrists to rope, throw, and tie off a calf tomorrow."

"I'm taking him to the hospital," Joann said.

"I'll come with you," Ty said. They rushed off.

That kind of put a damper on the night. We decided to go back to the hotel and watch a movie instead of staying at the rodeo.

No one blamed Mitchell for the accident. But Logan blamed himself. He was quiet the whole way back to the hotel. When we were in the elevator, he said, "Well, I feel just terrible. That was all my fault."

"You didn't make Cory fall," I said.

"But I brought Mr. Schwartz and Mitchell to the exhibitor area," Logan said. He held up his barn pass. "I was showing off."

"You were trying to make a little boy happy," I said.

"Which worked out great," Chloe said. "Thanks to you, Mitchell met his favorite rodeo rider."

"Thanks to me, Cory may not be able to ride tomorrow," Logan said. He sighed. "If he doesn't win, he won't be the Regional Champion."

Chloe and I sighed too.

Logan was right.

Chapter Eleven

One More Helper

We didn't take a tour of the trade show on Sunday. Logan didn't even ask if we wanted to go. Instead, he went to the rodeo with Chloe and me. When we got there, Joann was in the tack stall cleaning bridles.

"How is Cory's wrist?" Logan asked.

"It's not sprained," Joann said, smiling at us. "Cory is good to go."

"I am very glad to hear that," Logan said. He smiled back. Then he sat down on a folding chair. "What a relief."

"Would you girls take this bridle to Cory?" Joann asked. "He's in Laramie's stall."

"Do you want to come?" I asked Logan.

"No, thanks," Logan said. "I'll just be in the way."

I started to protest, but then I changed my mind. Logan was nervous around horses. Staying away was the smart thing to do. Still, it was too bad he didn't want to join in.

We found Cory quickly. "Hey!" I said as we walked up. "I heard you're all better. What a relief!"

"No kidding," Chloe said, smiling shyly. "I was so worried about you!"

"Aw, thanks, you two," Cory said. He winked at Chloe. "Did Joann send that bridle over?"

"Yeah, she did," I said. "It looks great."

"That bit sparkles!" Cory said when we handed him the bridle. He carefully hung it on a hook outside the stall.

"Laramie's coat is just as shiny," Chloe said.

"That's sweat," Cory said. "It's hot in these stalls. I'd better turn the fan on."

A box fan was hanging on a hook above the door. It pointed down into the stall. When Cory reached to turn it on, the fan fell. It hit the floor and stopped working.

"Oh, no. That's really bad," Cory said. "I don't want Laramie to get overheated, and we didn't bring a spare fan."

"We could run to a store for you and buy a new one," Chloe said.

"There's not enough time to find a store and get back before my event," Cory said. "Shoot. This is really bad news."

Suddenly, I had a great idea. "I'll be right back," I said. I picked up the fan and hurried back to the tack stall. I explained the problem to Logan.

"Can you fix it?" I asked hopefully.

"Let's see," Logan said. He took out his pocket knife. He used the screwdriver blade to gently open the motor casing.

I crossed my fingers, but I wasn't really worried. I knew Logan could repair every electrical device in our house. And I was right. He fixed the loose wire on Cory's fan.

"Here you go," he said, passing the fan to me.

"You should bring it to Cory," I told him. "He'll want to thank you in person."

Cory's eyes lit up when Logan brought the fixed fan back to Laramie's stall.

"Logan fixed it," I said. "I knew he could." I smiled up at my stepdad.

"Thanks, Logan!" Cory exclaimed. "You're a lifesaver."

"Glad to help," Logan said. "Good luck today. I have a feeling you'll do great."

Just then, another rider walked into the stall. "Could I borrow your clippers?" the man asked. "The cord on mine got cut in half."

"Sorry, Bruce, I didn't bring clippers," Cory said. "I trimmed our horses before we left."

Bruce sighed. "Then I'll have to ride a horse that needs a shave." He shook his head and added, "Knew I should've brought a spare."

"My stepdad might be able to help," I said.

"I think I can!" Logan said. He smiled and followed Bruce to his horse's stall.

A few minutes later, Bruce came back. "Your dad spliced the cord back together," Bruce told me. "These old clippers work as good as new. Thanks."

"You're welcome," I said, smiling. "Where's Logan now? Back at the tack stall?"

"Oh, he told me to let you know he had to go back to his trade show," Bruce said. "He said he'll see you later."

I didn't ask why Logan left. I thought I knew. Fixing things didn't make him feel like part of the rodeo crew.

Instead, it reminded him that he didn't fit in.

Chapter Twelve

For Luck

Logan came back an hour later and found me in the tack stall, waiting for Cory's event. Logan was all smiles.

"What happened?" I asked. "You look happy."

"Mr. Schwartz called me," Logan explained. "He heard about a deal on wire. I had to order at the trade show to get the super-low sale price."

"That's great!" I said. "You're having a pretty good day. You saved the fan, the clippers, and a ton of money for Granite Electric!"

"That's right!" Logan said. He grinned and gave me a hug.

Chloe ran into the stall. "Calf roping is starting!" she exclaimed.

We hurried out so we'd be able to watch. Chloe led us to an area where all of our friends were watching the event.

As we watched, the first calf shot out of a chute. A rider galloped after it and threw a rope around its head. When the boy jumped off, his horse kept the rope tight. The boy put the calf on its side and tied three legs with a smaller rope.

"That was fast," Jon said. "But Cory can do better."

Logan watched with great interest. He nudged me and showed me his crossed fingers when the announcer called Cory's name.

Cory was amazing. I barely had time to blink before he'd gotten the calf roped. None of us were surprised when he finished with the fastest time.

"Yahoo!" Jon yelled, waving his hat. "Cory won!"

Bulldogging was next, but we weren't as tense for Bobby's event. "Bobby doesn't expect to win," Jillian told us. "He just likes the challenge."

We cheered when Bobby jumped off his horse and grabbed the steer's horns. He wrestled it to the ground, but he didn't even come close to the fastest time.

The Regional Championship awards were presented after the bulldogging event. Cory was the best junior calf roper in the whole Midwest. He had his first silver belt buckle.

"That was amazing," Logan said once the show was over. He shook his head. "Those kids are talented!"

"Let's all have dinner together, Logan," Joann said. "I'm sure the kids want some time to say goodbye."

Logan glanced at me. I smiled. "Sounds good. We'll meet you in the café at six," Logan said.

* * *

The café was busy, so we couldn't get one big table. Logan sat with Ty and Joann. Chloe and I sat with Jillian, Jon, Cory, and Bobby.

"This was one of the best rodeo weekends ever," Jillian said. "I'm so glad we met you."

"Same here," I said. "I feel like we've known each other a lot longer than two days."

"Too bad it has to end," Cory said.

"It doesn't," Bobby said. "You've got phones."

Chloe squirmed. "I've also kind of got a guy at home," she said quietly.

Cory looked down. "He's a lucky guy," he said. He looked a little sad.

"Do you have a boyfriend?" Jon asked me.

"No," I said. Chloe shot me a look, but that was the truth. "Between school and horses and stuff I have to do at home, I don't have time," I explained.

"That's why Jon and Cory don't have girlfriends," Jillian said.

Jon nodded. "We're always either at school, or training, or going to rodeos," he said. "No time for girls, I guess."

"I solved that problem," Bobby said, putting his arm around Jillian. "I tangle with steers so I can be with her."

Jillian blushed. "That's not the only reason," she said.

"Yes, it is," Bobby said. He squeezed Jillian's shoulders.

"Most of the girls we meet don't ride," Jon said. "They just like hanging out with cowboys."

"Until one of them steps in horse manure," Cory said with a grin.

"That's why meeting you two was so great," Jon said. "You're not worried about that kind of thing."

"And you're not stuck up," Cory agreed.

"You helped out a lot," Bobby said. "We owe you!"

"And you guys like them," Jillian said, winking.

"Yeah. We like you," Cory admitted.

"Definitely," Jon said. He put his arm around me. "So, Monica," he said. "Can I get a goodbye kiss?"

"Just keep the dollar," I joked.

Chapter Thirteen

Heading
Home

The next morning, it was time for Chloe and Logan and I to head home. Once again, we got up super early. Chloe and I didn't have school, but Logan wanted to make it to Granite Electric for part of the day.

Chloe fell asleep after a little while in the car, so I sat up front with Logan. We listened to the radio for a while without talking.

Then Logan said, "You know, I meant for this to be a trip where you and I got to spend a lot of time together."

"I know," I said. "I'm sorry —"

Logan interrupted me. "You didn't let me finish," he said, smiling. "It was really cool to be able to hang out with you and Chloe, and to see you with the rodeo kids."

"So you're not mad that we didn't have more time together?" I asked.

Logan laughed. "No way," he said. "But you know how you and your mom have your special Saturdays? Maybe you and I could do that too, sometimes."

"I'd love that," I said.

"Maybe we could even go to some horse shows closer to home," Logan said.

"Really?" I asked. "You wouldn't be bored?"

"No way," Logan told me. "Now I get it."

"Okay," I said. "Then let's plan on it."

Then Logan got a worried look on his face. "I really don't want to ride any horses, though, okay, Monica?" he said.

I laughed. "As long as you don't make me spend a lot of time doing electrical work, I promise. No riding," I said.

"It's a deal," Logan said.

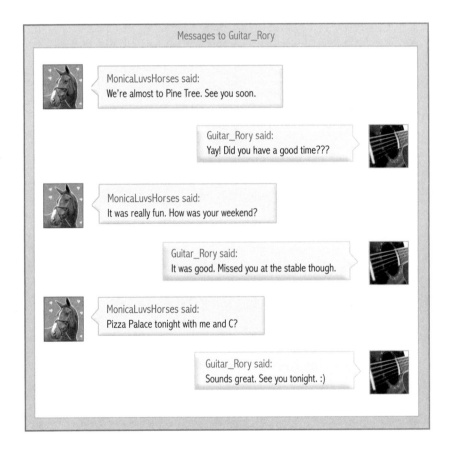

Messages to Guitar_Rory

MonicaLuvsHorses said:
We're almost to Pine Tree. See you soon.

Guitar_Rory said:
Yay! Did you have a good time???

MonicaLuvsHorses said:
It was really fun. How was your weekend?

Guitar_Rory said:
It was good. Missed you at the stable though.

MonicaLuvsHorses said:
Pizza Palace tonight with me and C?

Guitar_Rory said:
Sounds great. See you tonight. :)

Monica's SECRET Blog

Tuesday, 10:45 p.m.

I slept all day today because I'm still exhausted from our whirlwind weekend in Kansas City!

Once we got back, Logan and I dropped Chloe off at her house, and then we went home. Logan had to go to work for a while, but I went inside the house.

I was actually excited to see Angela. I bought her a headband at the Plaza, and she loved it. It was nice to see my mom, too. She took me aside and told me that she really missed me, and that her Saturday with Angela wasn't nearly as fun as it usually was with me.

A couple of hours later, I rode my bike to Pizza Palace. Chloe and Rory were already there. We ate and hung out for a while, but Chloe and I were both super tired.

Rory asked if we met anyone cool on our trip. I didn't want to lie, so we told him about Cory and Jon. I think he felt a little weird when Chloe said that Jon had a crush on me. So right away, I said, "He wasn't really my type."

And I think that made Rory feel better. I hope it did, anyway. Not that Rory and I are a couple. I just mean . . . you know. I guess I just mean that Jon isn't my type. But someone else might be.

Love,

Monica

 1 comment from Claudia: Sounds like you had a great time. I'm really glad you're back!!! Let's go to a movie tomorrow or something.

Leave a comment:

Name (required)

FRIEND BOOK

MONICA MURRAY

 AVATAR

SCREEN NAME: MonicaLuvsHorses

ABOUT ME:

View Photos of Me (100)

Edit My Profile

My Friends (236)

INFORMATION:

Relationship Status:
Single

Astrological Sign:
Taurus

Current City:
Pine Tree

Family Members:
Traci Gregory
Logan Gregory
Frank Jones
Angela Gregory

Best Friends:
Claudia Cortez
Becca McDougal
Chloe Granger
Adam Locke
Rory Weber
Tommy Patterson
Peter Wiggins

Activities: HORSEBACK RIDING!, hanging out with my friends, watching TV, listening to music, writing, shopping, sleeping in on weekends, swimming, watching movies . . . all the usual stuff

Favorite music: Tornado, Bad Dog, Haley Hover

Favorite books: A Tree Grows in Brooklyn, Harry Potter, Diary of Anne Frank, Phantom High

Favorite movies: Heartbreak High, Alien Hunter, Canyon Stallion

Favorite TV shows: Musical Idol, MyWorld, Boutique TV, Island

Fan of: Pine Tree Cougars, Rock Creek Stables, Pizza Palace, Red Brick Inn, K Brand Jeans, Miss Magazine, The Pinecone Press, Horse Newsletter Quarterly, Teen Scene, Boutique Magazine, Haley Hover

Groups: Peter for President!!!, Bring Back T-Shirt Tuesday, I Listen to WHCR In The Morning, Laughing Makes Everything Better!, I Have A Stepsister, Ms. Stark's Homeroom, Princess Patsy Is Annoying!, Haley Should Have Won on Musical Idol!, Pine Tree Eighth Grade, Mr. Monroe is the Best Science Teacher of All Time

Quotes: No hour of life is wasted that is spent in the saddle. ~Winston Churchill

A horse is worth more than riches. ~Spanish proverb

Mark my words

ambushed (AM-bushd)—hid and then attacked someone

boutiques (boo-TEEKS)—small shops that sell fashionable clothing or other specialty items

bribe (BRIBE)—offer a reward to persuade someone to do something for you

chandelier (shan-duh-LEER)—a light fixture that hangs from the ceiling and is lit by many small lights

champion (CHAM-pee-uhn)—a winner

compete (kuhm-PEET)—to try hard to outdo others at something

exhibitor (eg-ZIB-it-ur)—a person who is showing something to the public

goblets (GOB-lits)—tall drinking containers with stems and bases

obvious (OB-vee-uhss)—easy to see or understand

resented (ri-ZENT-id)—felt hurt or angry

sarcastically (sar-KAS-tik-lee)—with a bitter or mocking tone

sprained (SPRAYND)—injured a joint by twisting or tearing its muscles or ligaments

trade show (TRAYD SHOH)—a meeting of people who work in the same industry

volunteered (vol-uhn-TEERD)—offered to help

TEXT 911!

With your friends, help solve these problems.

Messages to Text 911!

1

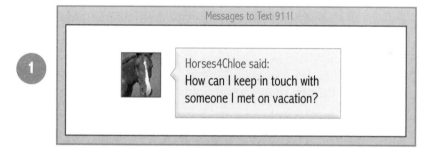

Horses4Chloe said:
How can I keep in touch with someone I met on vacation?

Messages to Text 911!

2

MonicaLuvsHorses said:
What happens if you like two people at the same time?

Messages to Text 911!

3

LoganElectric said:
How can kids and parents work on getting along?

You can write too.

Some people write in journals or diaries. I have a secret blog. Here are some writing prompts to help you write your own blog or diary entries.

1 I loved hanging out with Logan in Kansas City. Write about a time you did something special with a parent or another adult. What did you do? How did you feel about it?

2 Meeting Jillian, Bobby, Jon, and Cory was one of the highlights of my vacation. Write about a vacation you've gone on. Where did you go? What made it memorable?

3 I loved getting to see the rodeo. If you could go behind the scenes at an event, what would it be? Write about it!

ABOUT THE AUTHOR: DIANA G. GALLAGHER

Just like Monica, Diana G. Gallagher has loved riding horses since she was a little girl. And like Becca, she is an artist. Like Claudia, she often babysits little kids — usually her grandchildren. Diana has wanted to be a writer since she was twelve, and she has written dozens of books, including the Claudia Cristina Cortez series. She lives in Florida.

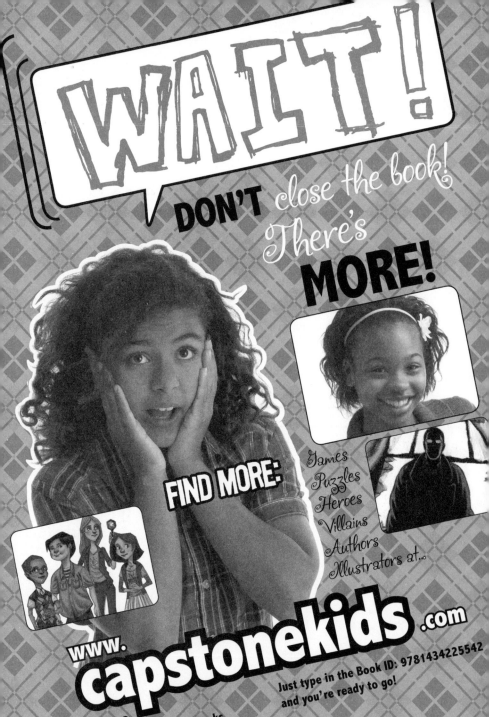